ONE THOUSAND TRACINGS

❖HEALING THE WOUNDS OF WORLD WAR II❖

LITA JUDGE

HYPERION BOOKS FOR CHILDREN
NEW YORK

Fossil Ridge Public Library District
Braidwood, IL 60408

For information address Hyperion Books for Children,
114 Fifth Avenue, New York, New York 10011-5690.
Printed in Singapore · First Edition · 1 3 5 7 9 10 8 6 4 2
Designed by Elizabeth H. Clark · This book is set in Caslon Antique.
Library of Congress Cataloging-in-Publication Data on file.
ISBN 13: 978-1-4231-0008-9 · ISBN 10: 1-4231-0008-5 · Reinforced binding
Visit www.hyperionbooksforchildren.com

For Elva, my mother
and Fran, my grandmother

———◆———

with special thanks to
Adi, Dave, and Namrata.

Papa Came Home
⌒ December 1946 ⌒

When I was three, Papa left home to join the war.

When I was six, the war was over,

and Papa came back to me and Mama.

I thought everyone we loved was home and safe.

But just before Christmas, a letter arrived that changed everything.

THEY HAVE NO SHOES
⤚Christmas 1946⤙

The letter was from our German friends, the Kramers.
We hadn't heard from them since before the war.

"They're starving," Mama said.
"Their clothing is worn. They have no shoes."
With tears in her eyes, Mama gathered wool socks, sweaters,
and her own winter coat. She placed all these things and
cans of meat, sugar, and tea in a box.
"It will be a very sad Christmas for many families
in Europe," she said.

DROPPED FROM THE HEAVENS
❧JANUARY 1947❧

Weeks passed, and another letter came.

> *When your package arrived, my wife suggested*
> *it was sent by the infant Jesus.*
> *It dropped from the heavens!*
> *You have no idea the excitement we shared*
> *when we all opened the parcel*
> *and took out each valuable treasure.*
> —*Dr. Kramer*

Below his name he wrote,
  Please send no more to me. Help others.

One Hundred Tracings

Dr. Kramer included a list of ten families.
He sent tracings of their feet.
Mama and I found a pair of shoes for each one.
I matched the shoes to the tracings.

Papa asked Dr. Kramer for more names.
And soon names came like rain,
pouring out of letters written in German.
Mama's grandma had taught her to read German.

Mama read a letter to me:
*We have only one pair of boots
and must take turns. I work at
night, and my husband works
during the day. We spend the
rest of the time in bed for
warmth.*

I counted one hundred foot tracings.
How would we find shoes for
everyone?

LATE NIGHTS
∾ MARCH 1947 ∾

Mama worked late nights, translating German letters into English.
She mailed the English copies to everyone we knew.
Soon, letters offering help came flooding back.
Our friends couldn't afford to send new shoes and clothing, but
perhaps they could send hand-me-downs.

Mama wrote so many letters.

In the evenings, we knitted wool socks
until our hands were raw.
I put the socks in the shoes,
on the tracings.

OUR BATTLES
∿ LATE MARCH 1947 ∿

The men had fought their battles during the war.

Now Mama and I fought our own battle.

A battle to keep families alive.

To keep them safe from cold and hunger.

Families we didn't even know,

yet we grew to love them.

Little boys and girls just like me, and they were suffering.

Mama and I searched for what they needed.

ELIZA
∽ APRIL 1947 ∽

Every week, more letters
arrived from Europe.

*Our home was bombed
and we lost everything.
My little girl and baby
boy and I lived in a cellar
with two other families for five
weeks, with only beans to eat. My husband is still
missing. Now we live with my father. Anything would
be helpful. My little girl, Eliza, has blond hair like
floating flax. Now she is pale and no longer plays.*

I thought about that little girl; she was my age.
I sewed a rag doll with a yellow dress
and slipped it into the pocket of a wool skirt we included
in the next package.
I wanted Eliza to have something nice.

ONE THOUSAND TRACINGS
ᴏᴥ June 1947 ᴥᴐ

Soon a thousand tracings
lined the walls and floors.
A thousand tracings waiting for shoes,
like rows of trees waiting for rain.
I imagined Eliza and her brother
barefoot.

BAREFOOT
∽ JULY 1947 ∽

All our friends helped.
Some families had less to give,
but always, they found a way.
Our neighbor, Mrs. Greenberg, canned and sold beans from her garden
to earn postage for the packages she sent.

Many children gave up their shoes.
It was summer, so we went barefoot.
We would get new shoes in the fall for school anyway.

Her Picture and Mine

Eliza's mother sent a letter.
A small note slipped out with a picture of a little girl.
Mama read the tiny, neat German script.

*Thank you so much for the little doll. I named her after you.
I lost my own doll when our home was bombed. But now
we have a nice home with Grandfather. Five other
families live here, but
everyone is friendly. Father
was a doctor during the
war, but we haven't heard
from him for a long time.*
—Eliza

Mama helped me write a
letter in German to Eliza.

HARD YEARS
∽ CHRISTMAS 1947 ∼

Winter was bitter cold.
Wind blew drifts that buried our windows,
and ice bent the birches and broke the pines.
Papa said, "Hard years sometimes come to trees as they do to men."

We waited to hear from Eliza again
and hoped her father had returned home for Christmas.
Finally, we received another letter from her:

*You should have seen Mama's face when she saw the soap
you sent. We haven't had enough soap to wash ourselves in
two years. I don't know if we were happier to take a bath or
drink a delicious cup of cocoa. My baby brother
loves his new blue trousers. He runs
through the house calling
himself a "Merikaner."
We have still not heard
from Father.*

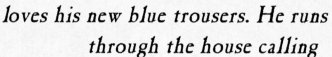

—Eliza

FEWER TRACINGS
∾ MAY 1948 ∾

Each day we searched for more shoes.
Mama and I found clearance sales, gathered unclaimed shoes
at repair shops, and collected them from neighbors.
I cleaned the used boots and put in new lacings.
Even old boots would be warm and sturdy.
We sent needles, tough thread, and leather for future repairs.

Fewer tracings now lined our floor.

Spring rains covered our fields
with yellow flowers
like ribbons on a present.

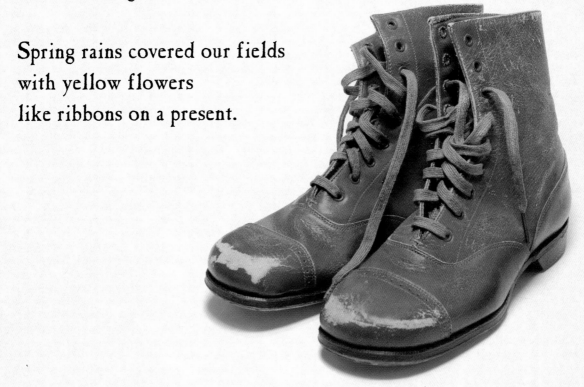

FATHER IS HOME
∼ OCTOBER 1948 ∼

Every day I checked the mailbox for a letter from Eliza.
Cold fall days turned trees to gold.
But just for a day, summer returned,
and Eliza's letter came.
Father is home!

Mama and Papa hugged me tight.
We danced and sang,
"Father is home! Father is home!"

RED SHOES

Eliza's father sent a beautiful painting of a swallow,
with instructions to hang it in my room.

The foot tracings were almost gone,
and life was returning to normal.

Papa gave Mama a pair of beautiful red dancing shoes.
Mama held them close.
She loved to dance.

❧ Author's Note ❧

I FOUND A DUSTY BOX while cleaning out my grandmother's attic. Inside were hundreds of aged, yellowed envelopes from all over Europe containing foot tracings of every size. My grandmother never spoke of this mystery. But when my mother saw the box, the memories crept back.

The aftermath of World War II brought great suffering to people in Europe. Thousands of Americans responded, healing the wounds of war with kindness. My grandparents, Fran and Frederick Hamerstrom, headed one relief effort initiated by American ornithologists. This is their story. They enlisted the help of fellow scientists, and together they sent care packages to more than three thousand people in fifteen countries throughout Europe.

The photos of people, letters, lists, and tracings shown in this book are actual items I found in the attic. The swallow painting now hangs in my house. Photos of canned food, boots, and soap are authentic to the 1940s, but are not the actual items sent. My mother made the rag doll used

DR. KRAMER

DR. LORENZ

in this book for me. I thought it represented beautifully all the toys she made and collected so many years ago for so many children.

Lasting friendships resulted from these acts of kindness. My grandparents became particularly close to Dr. Gustav Kramer and Dr. Konrad Lorenz, who later won the Nobel Prize. My mother and her brother even lived with the Kramer and Lorenz families for a year, and their children lived with my grandparents.

One letter found with the foot tracings read: "*We are full of thanks to our American colleagues; their friendship lets us believe once more in the future, which otherwise lay before us in frightful darkness.*"

DR. KRAMER'S CHILDREN

June 24, 194_

Dr. Helmut O. Hor_
Vienna I. Zoologische_ institut,
Leuger Ring 3
Austria

Mr.

Mrs.

...cal Club

...strom Tr.

...keney,   Mich.

...rith Dr_
...5,7, cle_
...d station t_
...e children

Sent to Hornberger_

1 man's heavy,
1 "   wool,
1 "   wool sh_

DIS FOR ADDRESS